Suggestions for Parents

First, read the book to your child. Allow him or her all the time needed to look closely at the pictures and to discuss the story. Then—even on another day—read the story again, now pointing to the words as you read them. After a few readings, the child who is ready to read will begin to pick up the often-repeated words—even the big ones! Before long (there's no hurry) the child will try to read the book alone. It is most important that you patiently build your child's confidence and give him or her the sense that reading is fun. You will find that there is nothing to match the excitement and satisfaction your child will feel on learning to read *a whole book*!

Eeeeeek!

By Patty Wolcott
Illustrated by Ned Delaney

Random House New York

Library of Congress Cataloging-in-Publication Data
Wolcott, Patty.
   Eeeeeek! / by Patty Wolcott ; illustrated by Ned Delaney.
     p. cm.—(Ten-word readers)
   Originally published: Reading, Mass. : Addison-Wesley, 1981.
   Summary: A lynx captures a fox, a hare, and a woodpecker
to make a stew, but then he falls asleep.
    ISBN 0-679-81929-0 (trade) — ISBN 0-679-91929-5 (lib. bdg.)
    [1. Animals—Fiction.] I. Delaney, Ned, ill. II. Title.
III. Series: Wolcott, Patty. Ten-word readers.
PZ7.W8185Ee 1991
[E]—dc20   91-12741

Fox and
Hare and
Woodpecker
Stew

1 Fox
1 Hare
1 Woodpecker
Salt
Pepper
Herbs

Fox and Hare and
Woodpecker stew.

Lynx caught Fox.

And Lynx caught Hare.

Eeeeeek!

Lynx caught Woodpecker.

Fox and Hare
and Woodpecker stew.
Hare and Fox
and Woodpecker stew.

Lynx slept.
Lynx slept
and slept
and slept.

And Woodpecker pecked.

Woodpecker pecked and pecked and pecked.

peck
peck
peck
peck

And Lynx slept.

Woodpecker escaped,
and Hare escaped,
and Fox escaped.

And Lynx slept.

10-Word Readers
by Patty Wolcott

Double-Decker Double-Decker Double-Decker Bus
Eeeeeek!
The Marvelous Mud Washing Machine
Pickle Pickle Pickle Juice
Tunafish Sandwiches
Where Did That Naughty Little Hamster Go?